HENRY'S LOLLIPOPS

A HENRY DUCK BOOK

ROBERT QUACKENBUSH

ALADDIN   NEW YORK   LONDON   TORONTO   SYDNEY   NEW DELHI

FOR PIET AND MARGIE,
AND NOW FOR EMMA AND AIDAN

ALADDIN
An imprint of Simon & Schuster Children's Publishing Division
1230 Avenue of the Americas, New York, New York 10020
First Aladdin hardcover edition May 2022
Copyright © 1975, 1987 by Robert Quackenbush
Originally published in 1975 as *Too Many Lollipops*
All rights reserved, including the right of reproduction in whole or in part in any form.
ALADDIN and related logo are registered trademarks of Simon & Schuster, Inc.
For information about special discounts for bulk purchases, please contact
Simon & Schuster Special Sales at 1-866-506-1949 or business@simonandschuster.com.
The Simon & Schuster Speakers Bureau can bring authors to your live event. For more
information or to book an event contact the Simon & Schuster Speakers Bureau at
1-866-248-3049 or visit our website at www.simonspeakers.com.
Designed by Tiara Iandiorio
The illustrations for this book were rendered in watercolor, pen, and ink.
The text of this book was set in Neutraface Slab Text.
Manufactured in China 0222 SCP
10 9 8 7 6 5 4 3 2 1
Library of Congress Control Number 2021946003
ISBN 978-1-5344-1549-2
ISBN 978-1-5344-1551-5 (ebook)

ONE SWELTERING SUNDAY,
Henry the Duck had a headache,
so he called his doctor.
The doctor told him to wear a woolen
bonnet and rest . . .

AND EAT A LOT OF LOLLIPOPS.

Out shopping on muggy Monday, Henry the Duck
was caught in a flash storm and got a sore throat.
The doctor told him to wrap a scarf around it
and rest . . .

AND EAT A LOT OF LOLLIPOPS.

Hanging pictures on torrid Tuesday,

Henry the Duck smashed a wing tip.

The doctor told him to put a mitten

on it and rest . . .

Mending his fence on wilting Wednesday,

Henry the Duck crushed a foot.

    The doctor told him to pull a stocking

over it and rest . . .

AND EAT A LOT OF LOLLIPOPS.

Setting the table on tropical Thursday,

Henry the Duck twisted his leg.

 The doctor told him to snap a garter

on it and rest . . .

AND EAT A LOT OF LOLLIPOPS.

Taking out the garbage on fiery Friday,

Henry the Duck mangled his tail.

The doctor told him to twist a bow

around it and rest . . .

AND EAT A LOT OF LOLLIPOPS.

That sizzling Saturday night, Henry the
Duck got a tummy ache.

The doctor told him to tie a pillow
on it and rest . . .